Ladybird Readers

Aladdin

Picture words

Aladdin

Aladdin's mother

princess

the king

magician

genie

palace

cave

well

smoke

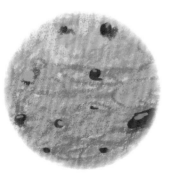

jewels

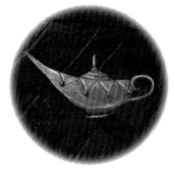

lamp

ring

Long ago, a poor woman and her son, Aladdin, lived in China.

One day, a man came. "Do you know Mustafa?" he asked.

"He was my father," said Aladdin, "but he's dead now."

"He was my brother," the man said. "So I am your uncle. I want to help you and your mother."

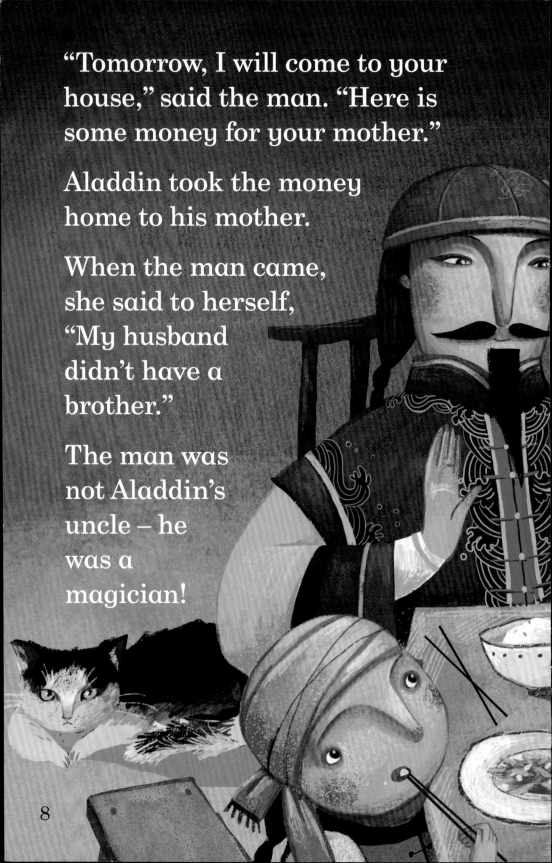

"Tomorrow, I will come to your house," said the man. "Here is some money for your mother."

Aladdin took the money home to his mother.

When the man came, she said to herself, "My husband didn't have a brother."

The man was not Aladdin's uncle – he was a magician!

The next morning, the magician took Aladdin shopping. He bought him some new clothes.

Then, they looked at big houses with lovely gardens.

"Let's sit and have something to eat," said the magician. "We have walked many miles today."

The magician gave Aladdin lots of cakes to eat. Then, he lit a fire. After Aladdin finished his food, the magician said, "Look over there."

Aladdin looked, and saw a ring on a big stone.

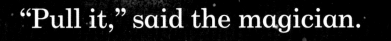

"Pull it," said the magician.

Aladdin pulled, and the stone moved. Then, he saw the top of a well. It was very dark inside.

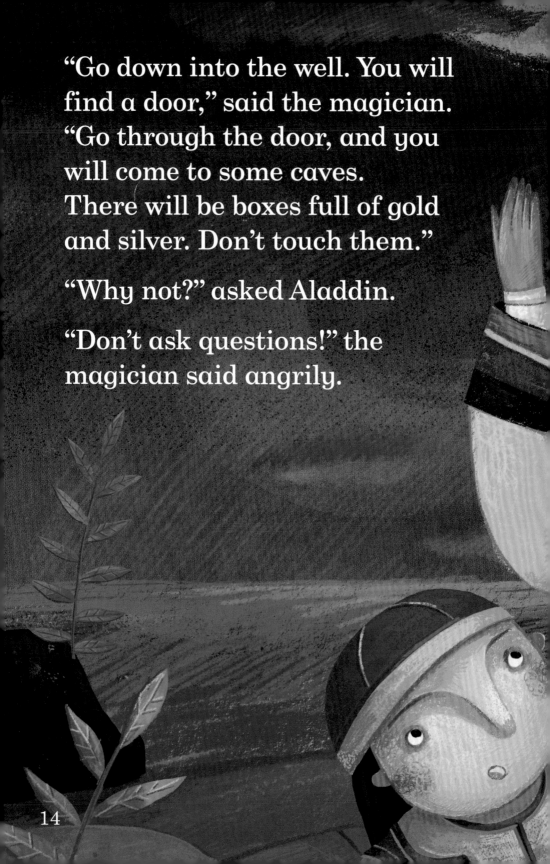

"Go down into the well. You will find a door," said the magician. "Go through the door, and you will come to some caves. There will be boxes full of gold and silver. Don't touch them."

"Why not?" asked Aladdin.

"Don't ask questions!" the magician said angrily.

"In the caves, you will see a garden. There will be a lamp in it. You can take things from the garden, but bring me the lamp," said the magician.

Then, he gave a ring
to Aladdin.

"This will help you,"
he said.

Aladdin climbed down
the well and went
into the dark caves.
He saw the boxes, but
he did not take any of
the gold.

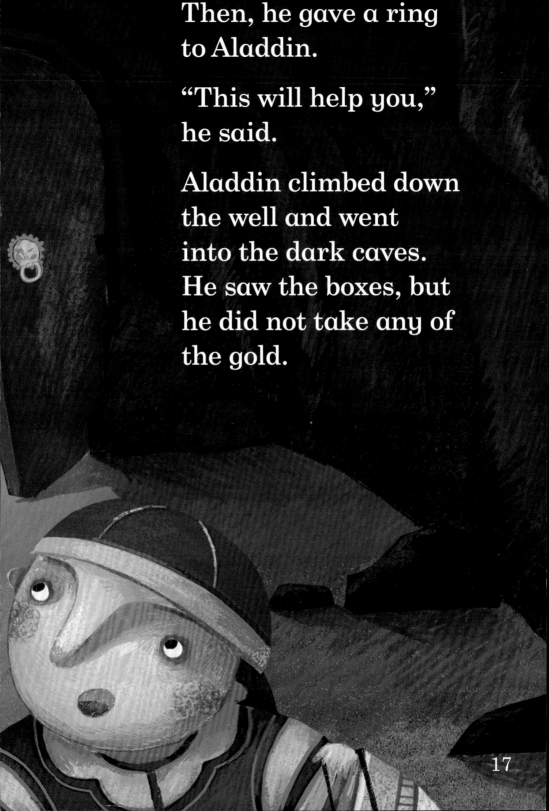

Aladdin walked into the garden.
Every tree was full of jewels!
Then, he saw the lamp.

Aladdin took as many jewels
as he could carry.

"I will come back," he thought,
"but first I must take this lamp
to my uncle."

When Aladdin climbed to the top of the well, he saw the magician.

"Help me out of this well, please!" Aladdin called.

"Give me the lamp first," said the magician.

"No!" Aladdin answered.

The magician was angry.
He said some magic words, and the stone moved over the well.
Aladdin was caught inside!

21

Aladdin sat down in the dark cave and cried. Then, he touched the magician's ring.

"I am the genie of the ring," he heard someone say. "The ring is magic. When you touch it with your finger, I will come to help you. What do you want?"

Aladdin closed his eyes. "Please take me home," he said.

Aladdin opened his eyes.
He was home!

"Where have you been?"
his mother cried. "There
is nothing for us to eat."

"I shall sell these jewels and
this lamp," said Aladdin.

"That lamp is old," said his
mother. "If I clean it, you will
get more money for it."

25

When Aladdin's mother cleaned the lamp, a strange man suddenly appeared.

"I am the genie of the lamp," he said. "When you touch the lamp with your hand, I will come and help you."

So, Aladdin said, "Please bring us some gold."

Suddenly, there were many beautiful gold plates.

"I will sell these plates," Aladdin said to his mother.

Three years went past. Aladdin became a handsome young man.

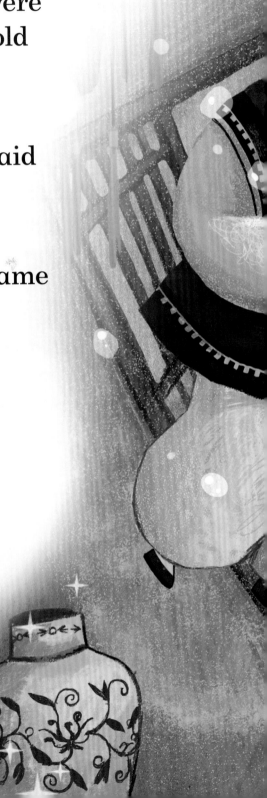

One day, Aladdin saw
a princess, and he fell
in love.

"I want to marry her,"
he thought.

Aladdin's mother went
to see the princess's
father, the king.

"My son wants to marry
the princess," she said.

"He can only marry
her if he is a rich man!"
cried the king.

31

Aladdin waited to hear his mother's news. Then, he went to find the princess.

"I love you," Aladdin told her.
"I am going to the palace to
speak to your father."

"Please take bags of gold to the king," Aladdin said to the genie. "Then, bring me expensive clothes and a beautiful horse. I am going to the palace."

Lots of people followed Aladdin to the palace.

The king looked inside the bags and said, "Now you can marry my daughter!"

35

The princess came to the palace.
Aladdin looked like a prince on
his horse, and she fell in love
with him.

Aladdin told the genie, "Make me
a beautiful house!"

Suddenly, there was a beautiful
house next to the king's palace.
Aladdin and the princess lived
happily for a year.

Then, the magician came back.

37

When the magician saw
Aladdin, he was very angry.

"I must take the magic
lamp from him,"
he thought.

The magician
bought some
new lamps.

Then, he walked along the streets shouting, "Bring me your old lamps. New lamps for old!"

"Aladdin has an old lamp," thought the princess, and she gave it to the magician.

As soon as the magician had the lamp, he touched it.

The genie came, and the magician said, "Take Aladdin's house away."

The next morning, Aladdin's house wasn't there, and the princess wasn't there!

"Where is the princess?" said the king to Aladdin. "You must bring her back!"

41

Aladdin touched his ring.
"Take me to the princess,"
he said to the genie.

Suddenly, he was with the
princess in his house. He gave
her a bag. She told him about
the old man with the lamps.

"That man is a magician," said
Aladdin. "Invite him to dinner.
I will hide behind the door.
Put this in his cup."

The princess did this.
The magician drank from the
cup, and soon he was sleeping.

"Make the magician go,"
Aladdin said to the genie.
Suddenly, the magician
wasn't there.

43

Then, Aladdin touched the lamp. "Take us home," he told the genie.

The king looked out of the palace window, and saw Aladdin's house.

"The princess is back!" he told the queen.

"Father, a magician took me, but he has gone now. Aladdin saved me," said the princess.

The king and queen smiled, and they all lived happily for many years.

Activities

The key below describes the skills practiced in each activity.

🖊 Spelling and writing

📖 Reading

💬 Speaking

❓ Critical thinking

✴ Preparation for the Cambridge Young Learners exams

1 Write the missing letters.

> agi   en   mo   ewe   in

1  m _agi_ cian

2  r _____ g

3 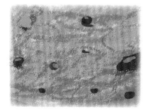 j _____ ls

4  g _____ ie

5  s _____ ke

2 Who says this? 📖 ✏️ ✪

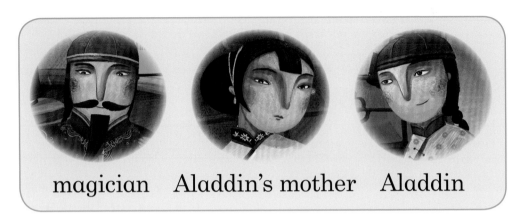

magician   Aladdin's mother   Aladdin

1 "I want to help you and your mother,"

said the .... *magician* ....

2 "He was my father,"

said ....

3 "My husband didn't have a brother,"

said ....

4 "Tomorrow, I will come to your house,"

said the ....

48

3 Read the questions. Write complete answers. 📖 ✏️ 🗯 ❓

1 Who was Mustafa, and what happened to him?

He was Aladdin's father.

He died.

2 Did Aladdin's mother believe the man? Why? / Why not?

3 What did the magician want from Aladdin, do you think?

49

4 **Look and read. Put a** ✓ **or a** ✗
in the boxes.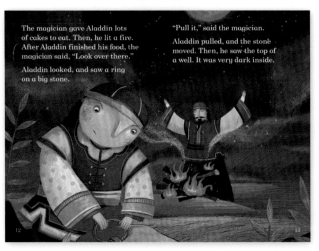

1 The magician cooked lots of meat
   on the fire for Aladdin to eat. ✗

2 The magician wanted Aladdin
   to go to the well. ☐

3 When Aladdin pulled the ring,
   the stone moved. ☐

4 Aladdin looked, and saw
   a jewel on a big stone. ☐

5 The well was very dark inside. ☐

5 Match the two parts of the sentences. Then, write them on the lines. 📖 ✏️

1 "Go down into

2 "Go through the door, and

3 "There will be

a you will come to some caves."

b boxes full of gold and silver."

c the well."

1 "Go down into the well."

2 _____

3 _____

1 What did Aladdin see in the caves?

(**a** a garden)

b a palace

2 What did the magician want from the garden?

a a box of gold and silver

b a lamp

3 What did the magician give Aladdin before he went down into the well?

a a lamp

b a ring

4 What did the magician say to Aladdin about the ring?

a "This will help you."

b "This will bring you money and gold."

7 **Look at the pictures. Talk to a friend about Aladdin.** 💬

What did Aladdin do?

Aladdin climbed down the well . . .

53

8 Read and write the correct form of the verbs. 📖 ✏️

When Aladdin climbed to the top of the well, he saw the magician.

"Help me out of this well, please!" Aladdin called.

"Give me the lamp first," said the magician.

"No!" Aladdin answered.

The magician was angry. He said some magic words and the stone moved over the well. Aladdin was caught inside!

20

When Aladdin (**climb**) climbed to the top of the well, he (**see**) .... the magician. Aladdin wanted to get out of the well. The angry magician (**say**) .... some magic words, and the stone (**move**) .... over the well. Aladdin was (**catch**) .... inside!

9 **Look and read. Write *T* (true) or *F* (false).**

Aladdin sat down in the dark cave and cried. Then, he touched the magician's ring.

"I am the genie of the ring," he heard someone say. "The ring is magic. When you touch it with your finger, I will come to help you. What do you want?"

Aladdin closed his eyes. "Please take me home," he said.

1 Aladdin touched the magician's ring while he was crying. _____T_____

2 Someone said, "I am the genie of the ring. The ring is magic." _____

3 The genie said, "When you touch the ring with your finger, I will take you home." _____

4 Aladdin asked the genie for a magic lamp. _____

10 Match the two parts of the sentences.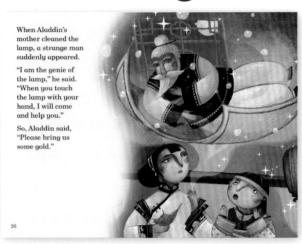

1 When Aladdin's mother cleaned the lamp,

2 "I am the

3 So, Aladdin said,

4 "When you touch the lamp with your hand,

a "Please bring us some gold."

b I will come and help you."

c genie of the lamp."

d a strange man suddenly appeared.

One day, Aladdin saw a princess, and he fell in love.

"I want to marry her," he thought.

Aladdin's mother went to see the princess's father, the king.

"My son wants to marry the princess," she said.

"He can only marry her if he is a rich man!" cried the king.

30

1 Aladdin saw a **genie,** / **princess,** and he fell in love.

2 Aladdin wanted to **marry** / **see** the princess.

3 Aladdin's mother went to see the **magician.** / **king.**

4 "My **son** / **genie** wants to marry the princess," she said.

5 "He can only marry her if he is a rich **man!"** / **magician!"** he said.

12 **Read the text. Choose the correct words and write them on the lines.** 📖 ✏️ ⬡

1	marry	married	were marrying
2	loves	was loving	love
3	tell	was telling	told
4	came back	came out	came into

1 "Now, Aladdin can ⎯⎯⎯ marry ⎯⎯⎯ my daughter!"

2 The princess fell in

⎯⎯⎯⎯⎯⎯⎯⎯⎯⎯ with Aladdin.

3 Aladdin ⎯⎯⎯⎯⎯⎯⎯⎯ the genie, "Make me a beautiful house!"

4 Aladdin and the princess lived happily for a year. Then, the magician ⎯⎯⎯⎯⎯⎯⎯⎯ .

13 **Read the answers. Write the questions.**

1 Why was the magician angry when he saw Aladdin?

He was angry because he thought Aladdin was dead.

2 Why

Because the magician hoped he could get Aladdin's old lamp.

3 Why

Because the princess did not know there was a genie inside it.

14 Do the crossword.

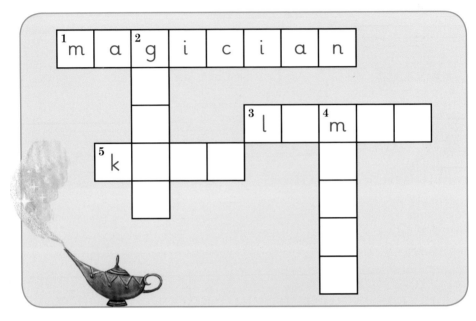

Across

1 This man said, "Take Aladdin's house away."

3 The magician bought some new . . .

5 This man wanted his daughter back.

Down

2 This man took away Aladdin's house.

4 The magician wanted to take the . . . lamp.

15 **Look and read. Choose the correct words and write them on the lines.** 📖 ✏️ ✲

Aladdin   genie   king   magician

1 This is the man who got
   Aladdin's old lamp.   the magician

2 This is the man who took
   away Aladdin's house
   and the princess.   ....

3 This is the man who said,
   "You must bring the
   princess back!"   ....

4 This is the man who told
   the princess, "Invite the
   magician to dinner."   ....

16 Order the story. Write 1—5.

_____ When Aladdin was a man, he fell in love with a princess.

___1___ When Aladdin was a boy, a magician gave him a ring, and sent him down a well to get a lamp.

_____ When the magician got Aladdin's lamp, he took Aladdin's house and the princess.

_____ When Aladdin's mother cleaned the lamp, the genie of the lamp came out and brought them gold plates.

_____ After Aladdin did not give the lamp to the magician, the genie of the ring helped Aladdin out of the cave.

17 Work with a friend. Talk about the two pictures. How are they different? 🗨

a

b

In picture a, the magician is with Aladdin and his mother.

In picture b, the magician is with the princess.

Level 4

The Pied Piper of Hamelin

978-0-241-25378-6

The Wizard of Oz

978-0-241-25379-3

Sam and the Robots

978-0-241-25380-9

The Little Mermaid

978-0-241-29874-9

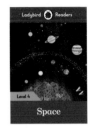

Space

978-0-241-25381-6

Pinocchio

978-0-241-28430-8

Alice in Wonderland

978-0-241-28431-5

Under the Oceans

978-0-241-29888-6

Knights and Castles

978-0-241-28432-2

Heidi

978-0-241-28433-9

Peter and the Wolf

978-0-241-28434-6

Dangerous Journeys

978-0-241-29891-6

A Fight with Underbite

978-0-241-29890-9

Sideswipe Loses his Head

978-0-241-29889-3

Aladdin

978-0-241-31606-1

Forests

978-0-241-31958-1

The Pony Games

978-0-241-31956-7